ALLIGATOR

LIZARD

DEER

DOG

EAGLE

SNAKE

RABBIT

MONKEY

JAGUAR

*Aztec & Maya
Pictograms*

VULTURE

NADJA SPIEGELMAN & SERGIO GARCÍA SÁNCHEZ

BLANCAFLOR

THE HERO WITH
SECRET POWERS

A FOLKTALE FROM LATIN AMERICA

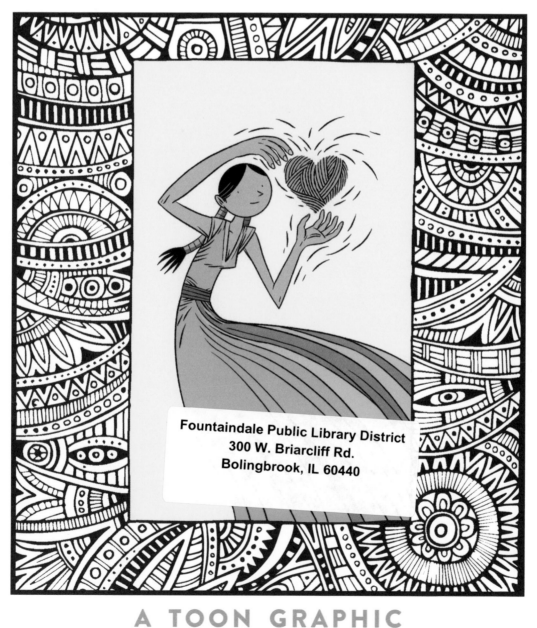

A TOON GRAPHIC

TOON BOOKS, NEW YORK

UPDATED FAIRY TALES FO

by F. Isabel Campoy

In Blanca Flor, Una princesa maya, *(illustration above by Rafael Yockteng,) the author, Victor Montejo, tells the story of Blancaflor as he heard it from his grandmother while growing up in Maya Jacaltec culture. The heroine is a Maya princess and her father, W'itz Ak'al, is a demigod, the Lord of the Forest.*

Why do we keep turning to folk and fairy tales from long ago? What can we get from reading about ogres and magic spells that is relevant to us today, to our lives in the age of the Internet? These tales have the power to open up our imagination. They resonate within our truest selves, the part of us that discovered the world when we were children and forms the core of who we are. A story like *Blancaflor*, which appears in many versions throughout Latin America, gives us a safe place to experience delight and terror in rapid turns while offering the promise of a happy ending. Folktales, passed down orally through generations, also show us the world by teaching us the customs, values, and cultural traditions of a people. Fairy tales may be populated by giants and talking stones, but they also take us into the homes of common folk solving real-life problems.

The Latin American heritage is richly diverse, a unique blend of Old World and New, spanning a continent across many geographic boundaries and cultures. When the Spaniards landed in the 15th century, they brought their medieval stories brimming with princesses and dragons. But since Spain is itself a land at the crossroads of many

TELL YOUR OWN STORY

It is part of the oral tradition for the performer to embroider the tale and make it his or her own. Storytellers like to use stock phrases to capture their audience's attention when they start and end their stories. Here are some of them, in Spanish and English:

¿Quieres que te cuente un cuento?
  Do you want to hear a story?

Había una vez.../ Érase una vez...
  Once upon a time...

Hace mucho tiempo...
  A long time ago...

Cuentan que...
The story goes that...

En un país muy lejano...
In a far-off land...

En la tierra del olvido, donde de nada nadie se acuerda, había...
In the land where all is forgotten, where no one remembers anything, there was...

...y colorín colorado, este cuento se ha acabado.
...and so, my fine-feathered friend, now the story has found an end.

...y vivieron felices para siempre.
...and everyone lived happily ever after.

From *Tales Our Abuelitas Told*, by F. Isabel Campoy and Alma Flor Ada

THE 21ST CENTURY

cultures, these tales already contained Catholic, Jewish, Arab, and Moorish influences. The Europeans' encounter with Maya, Aztec, Inca, and other Native American cultures–themselves spread widely across land and time–produced one of the world's most diverse and varied storytelling traditions. Everything that happens in the land of the popular *cuentos*, or fairy tales, was once invented by the pure magic of a storyteller's fertile imagination. As the stories grew and changed with every telling, the anecdotal became universal. Folktales often contain moral lessons; instead of telling us how to behave, they show us the implications of good and bad behavior. They also help us develop our social and emotional intelligence as we empathize with the different perspectives of the heroes and villains.

A recurring theme in the Latino experience is a celebration of strong women. Like so many *señoras* and *señoritas* in Hispanic families, the independent mothers, sisters, and daughters in these folktales have the inner strength to rise above obstacles and to overcome adversity. But above all, the reality of Latin American folktales is that, as in Blancaflor's story, magic is in all of us. Listen to this story and tell it to others: you, too, may discover that you have a secret power, the power of storytelling.

F. ISABEL CAMPOY and ALMA FLOR ADA are authors of many award-winning children's books, including *Tales Our Abuelitas Told*, a collection of Hispanic folktales that includes their version of BLANCAFLOR. As scholars devoted to the study of language and literacy, Alma Flor and Isabel love to share Hispanic and Latino culture with young readers. "Folktales are a valuable heritage we have received from the past, and we must treasure them and pass them along," Isabel says. "If you do not have roots, you will not have fruits."

Blancaflor was one of the stories included in the 1946 collection, Spanish Fairy Stories, translated by Gary Woolsey. In the illustration by Mario Hubert Armengold above, the prince travels on a winged horse.

Also by the same authors:
LOST IN NYC: A SUBWAY ADVENTURE
recipient of six starred reviews and many awards and distinctions, including a School Library Journal's Best Book of the Year and an American Library Association's Notable Children's Book

For Françoise –NS
For Alicia and Pablo –SGS & LM

Editorial Direction and Book Design: FRANÇOISE MOULY
Research Associate: MARÍA E. SANTANA
Endpapers, Aztec Designs and Motifs: GENEVIEVE BORMES
Colors: LOLA MORAL

SERGIO GARCÍA SÁNCHEZ'S & LOLA MORAL'S artwork was drawn and colored digitally

A JUNIOR LIBRARY
GUILD SELECTION

FOR VISUAL READERS
TOON
GRAPHICS

A TOON Graphic™ © 2021 Nadja Spiegelman, Sergio García Sánchez & TOON Books, an imprint of RAW Junior, LLC, 27 Greene Street, New York, NY 10013. TOON Books® and TOON Graphics™ are trademarks of RAW Junior, LLC. All rights reserved. No part of this book may be used or reproduced in any manner whatsoever without written permission except in the case of brief quotations embodied in critical articles and reviews.
Library of Congress Cataloging-in-Publication Data: Names: Spiegelman, Nadja, author. | García Sánchez, Sergio, 1967- illustrator. Title: Blancaflor, the hero with secret powers : a folktale from Latin America / Nadja Spiegelman & Sergio García Sánchez. Description: New York : TOON Books, 2021- | Includes bibliographical references. | Summary: "In this updated adaptation of a classic Latin American folktale, Blancaflor, a young ogre with magical powers, decides to secretly help a charming prince who has made a foolish bet with her father. Through saving the prince and the kingdom, she learns to be honest with herself and others about the things that make her special"-- Provided by publisher. Identifiers: LCCN 2021007309 Subjects: LCSH: Graphic novels. | CYAC: Graphic novels. | Fairy tales. | Ghouls and ogres--Fiction. | Princes--Fiction. | Magic--Fiction. | Ability--Fiction. | Fantasy. Classification: LCC PZ7.7.S65 Bla 2021 | DDC 741.5/973--dc23 LC record available at https://lccn.loc.gov/2021007309 All our books are Smyth Sewn (the highest library-quality binding available) and printed with soy-based inks on acid-free, woodfree paper harvested from responsible sources. Printed in China by C&C Offset Printing Co., Ltd. Distributed to the trade by Consortium Book Sales & Distribution, a division of Ingram Content Group; orders (866) 400-5351; ips@ingramcontent.com; www.cbsd.com. A Spanish edition, *BLANCAFLOR, la heroína con poderes secretos: un cuento de Latinoamérica*, is also available.
ISBN 978-1-943145-55-3 (hardcover English edition)
ISBN 978-1-943145-56-0 (softcover English edition)
ISBN 978-1-943145-57-7 (hardcover Spanish edition)
ISBN 978-1-943145-58-4 (softcover Spanish edition)
21 22 23 24 25 26 C&C 10 9 8 7 6 5 4 3 2 1
www.TOON-BOOKS.com

?!

GULP!

DON'T GET TOO ATTACHED TO THIS "PRINCE." BY THIS TIME TOMORROW, WE'LL BE EATING HIM FOR DINNER

WHADDYA MEAN, DADDY?

THIS PRINCE—HE THINKS LIFE IS ALL FUN AND GAMES. HA!

BUT ISN'T IT?

NO! LIFE IS **NOT** ABOUT FUN.

FIVE YEARS AGO, I CAST A GOOD LUCK SPELL ON THAT PRINCE—EVERY TIME HE PLAYS, EVERY TIME HE BETS, HE WINS.

NOW HE THINKS HE'S THE *LUCKIEST* MAN IN THE WORLD...BECAUSE **HE IS!**

THAT SEEMS AWFULLY NICE, HONEY. THAT'S NOT LIKE YOU AT ALL.

AH, BUT IT WAS ALL A TRICK! JUST LAST WEEK, I SENT HIM AN INVITATION TO COME TO OUR *CASTLE OF NO RETURN* TO PLAY THE HARDEST GAME OF ALL: **THE OGRE'S THREE!**

SHOW-OFF!

NOBODY LIKES A SHOW-OFF,
DEAR. YOU'LL NEVER BE ABLE
TO MARRY A PRINCE IF YOU
KEEP BRAGGING ABOUT YOUR
POWERS LIKE THAT.

WHO SAID ANYTHING
ABOUT WANTING TO
MARRY A PRINCE?

YEAH! MARRY HIM?
WE'RE GOING TO
EAT HIM!

♪ Encontré el ruiseñor. ♪
♪ que cantaba en la rama. ♪
♪ " Ruiseñor, o ruiseñor, ♪
♪ hacedme esta embajada, ♪
♪ din dirin din." ♪
♪ Din dirin din dirin din dirin daña, ♪
♪ din dirin din. ♪

22

♪" Ruiseñor, o ruiseñor,
♪ hacedme esta embajada,♪
♪ Y dile a mi amigo:♪
♪ que yo ya estoy casada, dindirindín." ♪
♪ Din dirin din dirin din dirin daña,♪
♪ din dirin din.♪

TIME TO SHOW OFF

by Nadja Spiegelman

The fairy tales that endure, that lodge themselves into our minds, are the ones that not only contain the symbols of a culture; they are the ones that speak to our deepest fears and emotions, to the basic foundations of our selves. In *Blancaflor*, a story blossomed about a girl who defies her father, who helps her lover with women's objects — a comb, a mirror, a bar of soap — a young woman who has the power to transform rocks into flour and then bread. Some version of this story, which follows the format of "The Girl as Helper in the Hero's Flight," exists in nearly every culture. It is one of the oldest and most widespread tales in the world. This story traveled from Norway to

Sergio García Sánchez (who illustrated this tale) and Lola Moral (who colored it) have two children who are also artists: **ALICIA GARCÍA MORAL** *(illustration above) and* **PABLO GARCÍA MORAL** *(illustration on the next page), who contributed here their own visual versions of* Blancaflor. *The family's cat is still working on his.*

Ireland, from Spain to the Americas. A similar story appears as "The Master Maid" in some cultures, and of course Blancaflor is cousin to Medea, the helper-maiden to Jason in his search for the Golden Fleece. In Latin America, the story of Blancaflor intermingled with Native and Maya tales and became canonical. In some indigenous cultures, the defiance of the ogre was understood as defiance of the landowners and of the Spanish conquerors. The moving of mountains and the flooding of plains echoed the skillful ways in which Indigenous Peoples developed agriculture and brought us so much of the food we eat today: corn and tomatoes and potatoes, beans and squash, among so many others. And yet, while rarely told directly as such, this story, in all its multicultural variants, has always been about the invisible labor of women.

Though much has changed, much has stayed the same, and I was drawn to this tale for its continuing resonance. One still earns far more on Wall Street, trading abstract futures, than as a teacher or a nurse or a mother raising children. Many women know about the sword of pain and the stone of sorrow. Most versions of this tale begin with the prince; my version begins with the girl. In this modern retelling, it is not enough for Blancaflor to discover her powers, to escape the murderous wrath of her parents, to be a helper to the hero. She must also escape from the surrounding patriarchy and learn to take credit for her accomplishments. Of course, women have magical powers. We have all known this since antiquity. Now, it's time for us to show them off.

ABOUT THE AUTHORS

The authors' other collaboration, Lost in NYC: A Subway Adventure, *received six starred reviews and many awards and distinctions, including a School Library Journal's Best Book of the Year and an American Library Association's Notable Children's Book.*

NADJA SPIEGELMAN is the Eisner Award-nominated author of the Zig and Wikki series of science comics for young children and the editor-in-chief of an international literary magazine. Her memoir *I'm Supposed to Protect You From All This* was published by Riverhead. She is a contributing editor at *The Paris Review* and the co-editor of the 2016-2017 project *Resist!*, a magazine of women's political comics and graphics.

SERGIO GARCÍA SÁNCHEZ, a professor of comics in Angoulême, France, and at the University of Granada, Spain, is one of Europe's most celebrated experimental cartoonists. His work has been published in over forty-five books and translated into nine languages. He lives in Granada with his wife and collaborator, **LOLA MORAL**, who colored the art for this book.

BIBLIOGRAPHY

The Dragon Slayer: Folktales from Latin America, Jaime Hernandez, TOON Books, 2017. *By the co-creator of the comic book series,* Love and Rockets. *Ages 8+*

Tales Our Abuelitas Told: A Hispanic Folktale Collection, F. Isabel Campoy and Alma Flor Ada (Authors), Atheneum Books for Young Readers, 2006. *Twelve stories from varied roots of Hispanic culture. Ages 5-10*

Latin American Folktales: Stories from the Hispanic and Indian Tradition, John Bierhorst, Pantheon Books, 2002. *A collection of Latin American stories sourced from twenty countries.*

The Monkey's Haircut and Other Stories Told by the Maya, John Bierhorst and Robert Andrew Parker (Illustrator), William Morrow and Company, 1986. *A collection of twenty-two traditional Maya tales.*

Fiesta Femenina: Celebrating Women in Mexican Folktales, Mary-Joan Gerson, Barefoot Books, 2001. *Eight stories of extraordinary women in Mexican folklore. Ages 8+*

Mexican-American Folklore, John O. West, August House, 2005. *A range of traditional Mexican-American proverbs, riddles, stories and folk songs.*

The Day It Snowed Tortillas / El Día Que Nevaron Tortillas: Folktales told in Spanish and English, Joe Hayes & Antonio Castro Lopez, Cinco Puntos Press, 2003. *A collection of New Mexican magical folktales for a modern audience. Ages 10-12*

Horse Hooves and Chicken Feet: Mexican Folktales, Neil Philip (Compiler) & Jacqueline Mair (Illustrator), Clarion Books, 2003. *Fifteen classic Mexican folktales. Ages 5-8*

Online Resources:
WWW.AMERICANFOLKLORE.NET *Retellings of folktales, myths, legends, fairy tales, superstitions, weather lore, and ghost stories from all over the Americas.*

WWW.SURLALUNEFAIRYTALES.COM SurLaLune *offers over 40 eBooks, including fairy tale and folklore anthologies, critical texts, poetry, and fiction.*

WWW.STORIESTOGROWBY.ORG *Folk & fairy tales from around the world.*

WWW.PITT.EDU/~DASH/FOLKTEXTS.HTML *Offers a variety of folklore and mythology texts, arranged in groups of closely related stories.*

HTTP://ONLINEBOOKS.LIBRARY.UPENN.EDU/ *An index of over two million books readable for free. (Search for subject: tales.)*

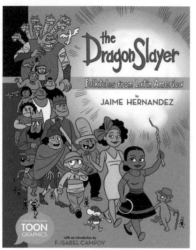

THE DRAGON SLAYER:
FOLKTALES FROM LATIN AMERICA
by Jaime Hernandez

FOR VISUAL READERS
TOON BOOKS®

TOON Graphics are comics and visual narratives that bring the text to life in a way that captures young readers' imaginations. When the authors are also artists, they can convey their creative vision with pictures as well as words. They can enhance the overarching theme and present important details visually along with the text. Reluctant and seasoned readers alike will sharpen both their literal and inferential reading skills. The award-winning collection covers many middle-grade curriculum themes such as Comparative Literature, Folktales, Greek Mythology, Diversity and Multiculturalism, Coming of Age, and Transportation, among many others. Deriving meaning from reading with the aid of visuals may be the best way to become a lifelong reader, one who knows how to read for pleasure and for information—a reader who loves to read.

LOST IN NYC: A SUBWAY ADVENTURE
by Nadja Spiegelman
& Sergio García Sánchez

THE WHITE SNAKE, based on
a fairy tale by the Grimm Brothers
by Ben Nadler

BLACK HEROES OF THE WILD WEST
by James Otis Smith
Introduction by Kadir Nelson

COMICS: EASY AS ABC!
by Ivan Brunetti
Françoise Mouly, *editor*

THESEUS and The Minotaur / ORPHEUS in The Underworld / OEDIPUS: Trapped By Destiny
by Yvan Pommaux

CAST AWAY ON THE LETTER A / THE WILD PIANO / THE SUSPENDED CASTLE
by Fred

HANSEL & GRETEL
by Neil Gaiman & Lorenzo Mattotti